Mr.
Macky is
Wacky!

Mr. Macky is Wacky!

Dan Gutman

Pictures by
Jim Paillot

■ HarperTrophy®
An Imprint of HarperCollinsPublishers

Mr. Macky Is Wacky!

Text copyright © 2007 by Dan Gutman

Illustrations copyright © 2007 by Jim Paillot

Library of Congress Cataloging-in-Publication Data is available.
ISBN-10: 0-06-114151-8 (pbk.) — ISBN-13: 978-0-06-114151-5 (pbk.)
ISBN-10: 0-06-114152-6 (lib. bdg.) — ISBN-13: 978-0-06-114152-2 (lib. bdg.)

Typography by Joel Tippie

❖

First Harper Trophy edition, 2007

18 19 20 BRR 31

To Emma

Contents

1 Crazy Pet Day   1

2 Mr. Macky's Fake Beard   10

3 If You Read This, You'll Go Blind   16

4 Abraham Lincoln's Face   23

5 George Washington's Face   28

6 It's Hard to Be the President   33

7 I Wish I Had a TV in My Pajamas   43

8 George Washington Vs.
Abraham Lincoln   49

9 Happy Presidents' Day   65

10 The President Is Missing!   72

11 President Wiggles,
Reporting for Doody   81

12 My Turn at Last   87

Crazy Pet Day

My name is A.J. and I hate school.

Man, I wish I was a grown-up. Grown-ups are so lucky. They don't have to go to school.

If I was a grown-up, you know which grown-up I would be? I would be the president of the United States. And you know what I would do if I was president of the United States? I would close all the schools. Then kids wouldn't have to go anymore. That's what I would do.

But until I become president, I guess I'll have to keep going to school. Bummer in the summer!

It was Crazy Pet Day at Ella Mentry School, so kids who had crazy pets brought them in to show the class. My friend Ryan brought in his hermit crab. This girl named Annette brought in her bird (which, if you ask me, isn't crazy at all). I don't have a crazy pet. I just have a dog, which isn't crazy at all. I wish I had a penguin. Penguins are cool. But my parents won't get me one because they live in Antarctica. Penguins, that is. Not my parents. My parents live at home with me.

"EEEEEEEK!" screamed this girl Emily, who cries over everything. "A rat!"

It wasn't a rat. It was a pet ferret that belonged to Neil Crouch (who we call Neil the nude kid even though he wears clothes).

But it *did* look a little bit like a rat. A long rat.

"What's your ferret's name?" I asked Neil the nude kid as I looked in his cage. (The ferret's cage, that is. Not Neil's. He doesn't live in a cage. He lives in a house with his parents.)

"His name is Mr. Wiggles."

Clap, clap, clap, clap, clap clapped our teacher Miss Daisy. That's her signal that we have to stop talking.

"We'll learn all about your crazy pets later," Miss Daisy told us. "But first, I have big news!"

"Miss Daisy said she has a big nose," I whispered to my friend Michael. He cracked up.

"Do you have something you'd like to share with the rest of us, A.J.?" asked Miss Daisy.

"No."

"The big news is that Presidents' Day is coming up next week," said Miss Daisy.

"What's Presidents' Day?" somebody asked.

"I have no idea," said Miss Daisy, who doesn't know anything. "Maybe one of you kids can tell the class what makes Presidents' Day special?"

I raised my hand. So did Andrea Young, this really annoying girl with curly brown hair. She was waving her hand in the air, like always. Andrea thinks she knows everything. But Miss Daisy called on me instead. So nah-nah-nah boo-boo on Andrea.

"Presidents' Day is special because we get the day off from school," I said. "Any time we get a day off from school, it's special."

Everybody laughed, even though I didn't say anything funny.

"Gee, I'm not sure that's right, A.J.," said Miss Daisy. "Can anyone else tell us what makes Presidents' Day special?"

Andrea and Emily were waving their hands in the air and moaning, "Oooooh!" like they were dying. They are so annoying. But Miss Daisy called on Michael, who never ties his shoes.

"Presidents' Day is special because that's the day big-screen TVs go on sale," said Michael. "My dad is gonna buy one. A really big one."

"Big-screen TVs are cool," I told Michael. The only thing better than watching TV is watching a big-screen TV.

"Hey," Ryan whispered to Michael, "can me and A.J. come over to your house and watch your big-screen TV?"

"Sure."

"You should get a screen so big that it's bigger than your house," I suggested.

"That's impossible," said Michael. "It wouldn't fit in the house."

"Who needs a house?" I said. "You

could just live inside the TV!"

I'm always coming up with genius ideas like that. That's why I'm in the gifted and talented program.

"Enough chitchat," said Miss Daisy. "I'm still waiting for somebody to tell me why Presidents' Day is special."

Nobody else raised their hand, so Miss Daisy called on Miss Smarty Pants I-Know-More-Than-You-Do. Why can't a bunch of presidents fall on her head?

"Presidents' Day is the day we honor—"

Andrea never got the chance to finish her sentence because at that very moment, the most amazing thing in the history of the world happened.

I'm not going to tell you what it was.

Okay, okay, I'll tell you. But you have to read the next chapter. So nah-nah-nah boo-boo on you!

Mr. Macky's Fake Beard

Hahaha! I knew you'd keep reading!

While Andrea was telling us why Presidents' Day was special, this tall, skinny guy walked into the class. He was wearing a dark suit, a big hat, and a really fake beard. And he was holding a can of chicken noodle soup.

"It's Abraham Lincoln!" shouted Emily, who looked like she just saw a

11

famous rock star or something. "He's my favorite president!"

I slapped my head. That girl Emily will fall for anything.

"Abraham Lincoln died like a million hundred years ago, dumbhead!" I told her.

"You're mean!" Emily said. Then she started crying and went running out of the room.

What a crybaby! All I did was call her a dumbhead, which she *is*.

Everybody knew the guy in the hat and beard was Mr. Macky, the reading specialist at Ella Mentry School.

"You're Mr. Macky!" Neil the nude

kid shouted.

"No, I'm not," Mr. Macky said in this really fake low voice. "The young lady was correct. My name is Abraham Lincoln. When I was a boy, I lived in a log cabin. We were so poor that I had to write on a shovel by candlelight."

"You're *not* Abraham Lincoln!" we all yelled. "You're Mr. Macky!"

"Okay, okay! I thought I could fool you."

Mr. Macky pulled off his hat and fake beard and tossed them on the floor. That's when the most amazing thing in the history of the world happened.

Emily came back in the room!

Well, that wasn't the amazing part. Emily comes back in the room all the time. The amazing part was that when she came back, Emily stepped on Mr. Macky's fake beard.

"EEEEEEEEEEEK!" she screamed. "A rat!"

Emily slipped and fell. She was on the floor, freaking out. It was hilarious. We were all cracking up.

"It's not a rat," I told Emily. "It's just Mr. Macky's fake beard, dumbhead!"

Emily started crying and went running out of the room again.

She's weird.

If You Read This, You'll Go Blind

Mr. Macky was reading that soup can he brought into our class.

"I love to read," said Mr. Macky. "Don't you?"

"Yeah!" said all the girls.

"No!" said all the boys.

Mr. Macky is always trying to get us to

read. What is his problem? Doesn't he know that reading is a big bore? Why are you even reading this book? If I were you, I'd be doing something worthwhile, like watching a big-screen TV. The only books worth reading are Dr. Seuss books. He was cool.

My friend Billy who lives around the corner told me that if you read too much, you'll go blind. Homework involves a lot of reading. So, just to be on the safe side, I'm going to stop doing my homework so I won't go blind.

"Mr. Macky, why do you have a can of chicken noodle soup?" asked Michael.

"I was reading the label," he said.

"Reading can take you on a journey."

"So can watching TV," I said.

"Yes, but you can learn so much more by reading," said Mr. Macky, "because you can use your imagination. I'll read anything."

"But what can you learn from a soup can?" asked Ryan.

"I learned that chickens have noodles," said Mr. Macky.

"Chickens have fingers, too," said Michael. "My mom gives me chicken fingers for lunch all the time."

"Chickens have nuggets, too," I added.

"They do not," said Andrea.

"Do too," I told her.

"Do not."

We went back and forth like that for a while.

"Let's discuss chickens some other time," said Miss Daisy. "I think Mr. Macky

is here to talk about Presidents' Day."

"Right you are," said Mr. Macky. "I had an idea to promote reading at Ella Mentry School. In celebration of Presidents' Day, we're going to read all about the presidents. We're going to learn a lot. Each of you is going to give an oral report* on a president. You'll even get to dress up as your president. The whole school will be involved. Doesn't that sound like fun?"

"Yeah!" said all the girls.

"No!" said all the boys.

———————————————

*Oral means "mouth," so an oral report comes out of your mouth. Only gifted and talented kids know hard words like that.

Why is it that girls always want to read books, learn stuff, give reports, and play dress-up? What is their problem? Girls are weird.

How come we never celebrate anything by sitting around and watching big-screen TVs?

"I think it's a *great* idea," said Miss Daisy (a girl, of course). "I don't know anything about the presidents."

Of course not. Miss Daisy doesn't know anything about *anything*. I can't believe she got a job as a teacher.

"I think it's a great idea too," said Andrea, the big brownnoser. "When did you get this great idea, Mr. Macky?"

"Four score and seven years ago," he replied.

"I can't wait to get started on my oral report!" Andrea said, all excited. "I'm going to work really hard and do the best job I can."

"Can you possibly be any more boring?" I asked her.

"I have to go now," Mr. Macky said, "because I have a lot of things to read. I have to read the newspaper. Then I have to read the back of the cereal box. Then I have to read the graffiti in the bathroom. Then I have to read the phone book."

That guy sure loves reading. He's weird.

Abraham Lincoln's Face

"Who can tell us something about the *real* Abraham Lincoln?" Miss Daisy asked after Mr. Macky left with his hat and beard.

"*Lincoln* rhymes with *stinkin'*," I said.

"True. . . ."

"Abraham Lincoln's face is on the penny," said Andrea.

"That's right!" said Miss Daisy. Andrea looked all proud of herself. I hate her.

"He should take that penny off his face," I said.

"No," Andrea said, "I mean his face is *on* the penny."

"How did he hold the penny on his face?" Ryan asked. "With glue?"

"That's disgusting," said Michael. "I wouldn't put glue on *my* face."

"He was probably trying to cover up his pimples," I told them. "When my big sister has pimples, she won't even go outside."

"Enough chitchat," said Miss Daisy, clapping her hands again. "Let's look at our crazy pets now."

I still say Abraham Lincoln was weird to put pennies on his face.

We took some of the animals out of their cages and looked at them. Ryan told us about his hermit crab. Hermit crabs are really boring. They don't do *anything*! You can hardly even tell when they die, because they do the same stuff dead that they did when they were alive. Nothing! Hermit crabs are weird.

Annette told us about her bird. It was boring too, because it didn't talk or anything. The only cool birds are the ones that talk.

Neil the nude kid told us about his ferret. He said ferrets have really bad eyesight and they poop when they get excited. We all said we'd try not to get Mr. Wiggles excited. Everybody thought he was cool, even if he looked sort of disgusting.

Emily said she's allergic to the ferret's fur. It makes her cough and rub her eyes.

"Ferrets are gross, anyway," she said.

"Mr. Wiggles looks like a long rat."

I was going to say, "So does your face," but Emily would probably run out of the room crying again. Then I'd have to go to the principal's office. Besides, she was right. Mr. Wiggles *did* look like a long rat. But if you ask me, ferrets are cool. Not as cool as penguins, but they're still cool.

George Washington's Face

We were having fun learning about our crazy pets. But guess who suddenly walked into the door?

Nobody! Because if you walked into a door, you would hurt your head. But guess who walked into the class?

It was some funny-looking guy all dressed up in a fancy army uniform. He had a white wig on his head and a sword in his hand.

"It's George Washington!" said Miss Daisy, all excited. She stood up and gave him a salute.

We all knew it wasn't George Washington. It was just Mrs. Roopy, our librarian. She is always pretending to be somebody else. One time she pretended to be Johnny Appleseed, and she walked around all day with a pot on her head. I still don't understand why you have to wear a pot on your head to plant apples.

Mrs. Roopy is loopy.

"You're not George Washington!" we all shouted. "You're Mrs. Roopy, the librarian!"

"You must be mistaken," Mrs. Roopy said in a fake low voice. "I was the first president of the United States. I cannot tell a lie. I chopped down a cherry tree. I have wooden teeth. See?"

Mrs. Roopy took out her teeth. It was disgusting. I was glad when she put those gross teeth back in her mouth.

"I came to tell every- one that when you come to the library, you'll find lots of books

about me and the other presidents, too,"
said Mrs. Roopy. "They'll help you pre-
pare for your Presidents' Day oral reports.
I wish I could hang around and tell you
more, but I must go to fight the British."

She ran out of the room.

"That was totally Mrs. Roopy," said
Ryan.

After Mrs. Roopy left, Miss Daisy asked,
"Who can tell us something about the
real George Washington?"

"His face is on the dollar bill," said little
Miss See-How-Smart-I-Am Andrea.

"That's right!" said Miss Daisy. Andrea
looked all proud of herself.

"He should take that dollar bill off his
face," I said.

"No, I mean his face is *on* the dollar bill."

I knew perfectly well what Andrea meant. I was just yanking her chain.

"How could George Washington fight the British with that dollar bill on his face?" I asked.

"Yeah," Michael said. "Why didn't he just carry the dollar bill in his wallet like a normal person?"

"Enough chitchat. It's time for reading," Miss Daisy told us. "Let's read a book by my favorite author, Dr. Seuss."

She read us a story called *Yertle the Turtle*. It was pretty cool.

But I still say George Washington was weird.

It's Hard to Be the President

The next day Mr. Macky popped his head in our class right after the morning announcements.

"Are you all getting excited about Presidents' Day?" he asked.

"Yeah!" said all the girls.

"No!" said all the boys.

"I have a question for you," Mr. Macky said. "What color is the White House?"

Everybody waved their hands around in the air. Even the dumbest dumbbell in the world knows the White House is white. That's why they call it the White House. *Duh!*

But Mr. Macky didn't call on any of us. Instead, he called on Miss Daisy, who was waving her hand just like she was a kid.

"The White House is blue, right?" said Miss Daisy.

I slapped my head. She doesn't know *anything*!

"The White House is *white!*" we all shouted.

"Oh," said Miss Daisy. "I thought it was a trick question."

Miss Daisy is crazy. She is the dumbest teacher in the history of the world.

"To what do we owe the pleasure of your company, Mr. Macky?" asked Miss Daisy. (That's grown-up talk for "What are *you* doing here?")

"I thought I would tell the students a little bit about the presidents," said Mr. Macky. "It might help them decide which president to choose for their oral reports."

"Excellent idea!" Miss Daisy said as Mr. Macky went running out of the room.

"Where did he go?" asked Ryan.

"Who knows?" I said. "He's weird."

Mr. Macky came right back in, but this time he was walking on his knees. And he had his shoes over his knees, so it looked like he was really tiny.

"I'm James Madison," Mr. Macky said. "I am the 4th president—and the shortest. I'm about five feet four inches tall and I only weigh one hundred pounds."

"What a shrimp!" Ryan said.

Mr. Macky excused himself and ran out of the room again. Then he came back with a cigar in each hand, a cigar in his mouth, and two cigars sticking out of his ears.

"Who are you now?" asked Andrea.

"I am Ulysses S. Grant," Mr. Macky said. "The 18th president. I smoke twenty cigars a day."

"That's disgusting!" said Michael.

Mr. Macky ran out of the room again. He must have stuffed a bunch of pillows under his shirt, because when he came back in, he was really fat. Nobody can gain weight that fast.

"Who are you now?" asked Emily.

"I'm William Howard Taft," he said, "the 27th president. I weigh more than three hundred pounds. I had a special bathtub built for me in the White House."

"You should go on Weight Watchers," I said. "My mom lost twenty pounds that way."

Mr. Macky ran out of the room again. When he came back this time, he was wearing a dress!

"Who are you *now*?" asked Ryan.

"I'm Franklin D. Roosevelt," he said, "the 32nd president. My mother made me wear a dress until I was five years old."

"Your mother was weird," I said.

Mr. Macky ran out of the room *again*. When he came back, he wasn't wearing any clothes at all. He just had a towel wrapped around him!

"Who are you *now*?" asked Michael.

"I'm John Quincy Adams. The 6th president. I like to go skinny-dipping in the Potomac River near the White House."

"You're *really* weird!" I said.

Mr. Macky kept running in and out of the room over and over again. Each time he came back, he was dressed up like a different president—Jefferson, Reagan, Kennedy, Jackson. It went on and on and on.

We learned a lot of important stuff about

the presidents, like which one grew the first tomatoes in America (Jefferson) and which one was a member of the Beatles (Harrison). Most of them were weird.

Did you know that Andrew Johnson, the 17th president, never went to school? It's true! He didn't even learn to read until he was seventeen years old. See? That just proves that any dumbhead can grow up to be president.

Finally Mr. Macky stopped running in and out of the room. He was panting and gasping for breath.

"Being president is a *very* hard job," he said.

"Who is your favorite president, Mr. Macky?" asked Andrea, who never misses the chance to brownnose a grown-up.

"Hmm," said Mr. Macky, rubbing his chin where his fake beard used to be. "That's a hard one. I think my favorite is Millard Fillmore. He was the 13th president.

MILLARD FILLMORE???

Can you believe that? The guy's name was really *Millard Fillmore*! He must have been a great man. Anyone who could become president even though his name was Millard Fillmore *must* have been a great man. I know that if *my* name was Millard, kids would make fun of me all day long. I'd have to move to Antarctica.

"You know what I like best about

Millard Fillmore?" Mr. Macky asked us. "His name!"

Then he started writing on the blackboard:

Millard Fillmore

Fillard Millmore

Moremill Fillard

Lardfill Moremill

Millfill Morelard

Lardmore Fillmill

He went on and on like that until it was time for lunch.

Mr. Macky is wacky!

7

I Wish I Had a TV in My Pajamas

We went to the vomitorium for lunch. I sat with Ryan and Michael. Andrea and her annoying friend Emily were at the next table.

I had a peanut butter and jelly sandwich. Michael had a ham sandwich. Ryan had a wichsand, which is a sandwich with the meat on the outside and the bread in the middle. Ryan invented the wichsand. He should get the No Bell Prize.

"Which president are you gonna be for your oral report?" Michael asked.

"I'm gonna be James Garfield," Ryan said, "because I like Garfield the cat."

"I'm gonna be Herbert Hoover," said Michael, "because he was named after a vacuum cleaner."

"I think the vacuum cleaner was named after *him*," I said.

"What about you, A.J.," asked Ryan. "Which president are you gonna be?"

"I don't know yet," I told the guys. "But it would be cool to be president for *real*.

Nobody can tell him what to do! I'll bet the president can stay up late, even on school nights."

"I'll bet he can eat candy anytime he wants," Ryan said. "And he doesn't have to brush his teeth."

"I'll bet he doesn't even have to make his bed," I said, "or clean up his room or feed his fish."

"I'll bet he can watch TV in his pajamas all day if he feels like it," Michael said.

"The president has a TV in his pajamas?" I asked. "That's cool!"

I noticed that Andrea and Emily kept turning around and giggling. Girls are always giggling. Andrea and Emily were probably talking about girly stuff like smelly perfume and how many pairs of shoes they have. We boys have more important stuff to talk about, like whether or not the president has a TV in his pajamas.

We ignored them. Our conversation was none of their beeswax anyway.

"Do you think Mr. Macky was telling the truth when he said Abraham Lincoln had to write on a shovel?" I asked the guys.

"Lincoln should have used a computer," said Ryan. "It's much easier to write on."

"Yeah, but you can't use a computer to dig a hole," Michael pointed out.

"Well, you can't check your e-mail on a shovel," Ryan said.

"You could check your e-mail if you had a shovel with a built-in computer," I told them.

The lunch lady, Ms. LaGrange, told us it was time to clean off our trays. Andrea and Emily walked by our table.

"Boys are dumbheads," Andrea said.

George Washington Vs. Abraham Lincoln

It was the Friday before Presidents' Day, and we were putting our stuff into our cubbies. I heard Andrea tell Emily that she was nearly finished with her Presidents' Day oral report. She picked John F. Kennedy as her president.

"I bet my report is going to be the best

in the whole class," Andrea whispered to Emily.

Whenever we have an assignment to do, Andrea's is *always* the best in the class. Why does she have to be best every single time? I hate her.

After we pledged the allegiance, we had to go to the all-purpose room for an assembly. Mr. Klutz was up on the stage. He's the principal of the school, and his head is completely bald. I mean *completely*. I wrote a poem about Mr. Klutz. It goes like this:

> *His head is bare.*
>
> *It looks like a pear.*
>
> *His hair is not there.*

Where is his hair?

Maybe it's in his chair.

Someone should share their hair.

It's not fair!

But I don't care.

I wish I had a chocolate éclair.

Did you like my poem about Mr. Klutz's hair that he doesn't have? I tried to sound like Dr. Seuss. He was cool, even if he wasn't a real doctor.

Anyway, being the principal is like being the president of Ella Mentry School. I guess *every* day is Presidents' Day for Mr. Klutz. He told us he was getting excited about the big holiday on Monday.

"Are you going to buy a big-screen TV, Mr. Klutz?" Michael shouted.

"No, why?" he asked.

"Because they go on sale on Presidents' Day," Michael said. "My dad is going to buy one."

Mr. Klutz told us he was more interested in the presidents than big-screen TVs.

"In honor of Presidents' Day," Mr. Klutz announced, "we're going to have you kids vote for the president of Ella Mentry School. Whoever gets the most votes will be the president when we get back to school after the holiday. That's how democracy works. Any questions?"

"Can we vote for any president we want?" one of the third graders asked.

"There will be two candidates," Mr. Klutz said. "I would like to introduce them to you now. Each president will make a short speech, and then we will vote."

Mr. Macky and Mrs. Roopy walked up onto the stage dressed like Abraham Lincoln and George Washington. Everybody clapped. The presidents each took a bow. Mrs. Roopy spoke first.

"My name is George Washington," she said. "I was the first and best president! I was the father of our country. I defeated the British in the Revolutionary War.

Vote for me."

Everybody clapped. Then Mr. Macky stepped forward to give his speech.

"My name is Abraham Lincoln. I was the 16th president. I saved the Union. I freed the slaves. I wrote the Gettysburg Address. Vote for *me*!"

Everybody clapped.

"Okay!" said Mr. Klutz. "Do either of you gentlemen have anything to add?"

"I would just like to mention that the George Washington Bridge was named after me," said Mrs. Roopy.

"Well, the Lincoln Tunnel was named after *me*," said Mr. Macky. "And Lincoln Logs, too."

George Washington—I mean, Mrs. Roopy—laughed.

"They named some *logs* after you?" she said. "Big whoop! They put *me* on the dollar bill."

"Oooooh!" went all the kids.

"Oh yeah?" said Mr. Macky. "I'm on the *five*-dollar bill. So I must be *five* times

better than you."

"Oooooh!" went all the kids. Abraham Lincoln totally dissed George Washington! In his face!

"I cannot tell a lie," George Washington said. "You're ugly."

"Oooooh!" went all the kids.

Abraham Lincoln looked really mad. I thought the two of them were going to start fighting! But Mr. Klutz stepped in between them.

"Gentlemen! Gentlemen!" he said. "There's no need to get nasty here. Remember, Benjamin Franklin is on the *hundred*-dollar bill. Does that mean he's better than both of you?"

The two presidents looked at Mr. Klutz.

"Who asked you?" said Abraham Lincoln as he shoved Mr. Klutz out of the way.

"Oooooh!" went all the kids.

"The Washington Monument is *way* taller than the Lincoln Memorial," George Washington told Abraham Lincoln.

"You have wooden teeth!" Abraham Lincoln told George Washington. "And you probably wear that silly wig to hide your bald spot!"

"Oooooh!" went all the kids.

"I refuse to fight," said George Washington. "I am a peace-loving man."

"Nobody loves peace more than I do,"

said Abraham Lincoln.

"Oh yeah?" said Washington. "You want to fight over who loves peace the most?"

"Oooooh!" went all the kids.

"Bring it on, old man!" said Lincoln. "I'll kick your butt!"

I couldn't believe Abraham Lincoln

said "butt"!

The next thing we knew, both presidents started fighting! George Washington put Abraham Lincoln in a headlock! Then Abraham Lincoln picked George Washington up over his head and started spinning him around! Soon the two of them were fighting on the floor.

It was cool. You should have been there. All the kids started cheering and yelling. It was just like watching professional wrestling on a big-screen TV.

"Break it up!" shouted Mr. Klutz as he separated the two presidents. "Calm down, both of you! You should be ashamed of yourselves. Go to my office."

Wow! Kids get sent to the principal's office all the time, but that was the first time I ever saw a *grown-up* get sent there.

Finally everybody calmed down. It was time to vote for the president of Ella Mentry School. Miss Daisy and the other teachers passed out pieces of paper and pencils. We were told to write WASHINGTON or LINCOLN on our paper.

"Whoever gets the most votes will be the president of Ella Mentry School," announced Mr. Klutz. "The majority rules. That's what democracy and fair elections are all about."

Hmm. George Washington and Abraham Lincoln were both pretty cool guys.

I couldn't make up my mind which one to vote for.

That's when I got the greatest idea in the history of the world! I decided I wasn't going to vote for *either* of those guys. I took my piece of paper and wrote this:

I VOTE FOR MR. WIGGLES.

I passed my paper over to Neil the nude kid. Neil giggled and passed my paper over to Ryan. Ryan giggled, and *he* passed my paper over to Michael. They passed my paper all the way down the row so our whole class saw it. I don't know what happened to it after that, but there was a lot of giggling in the all-purpose room.

"If everybody is finished voting," said Mr. Klutz, "please pass your papers to your teachers so they can tally up the votes."

We passed our papers to Miss Daisy, and she counted the votes for our class. Mrs. Patty, the school secretary, came out of the office with a calculator. Each teacher told Mrs. Patty how her class voted, and Mrs. Patty added up the votes. It took about a million hundred minutes. Finally she handed a piece of paper to Mr. Klutz.

"And the president of Ella Mentry School is . . . *Mr. Wiggles*?"

All the kids started yelling and

screaming and cheering. Neil the nude kid's pet ferret was the new president of Ella Mentry School!

"Hooray for Mr. Wiggles!" we all shouted. "Hip hip hooray!"

Happy Presidents' Day

Monday is usually the worst day of the week, because it means we have five days of school in a row. But not *this* week. It was Presidents' Day. No school on a Monday! Hooray!

Now, you're not going to believe this in a million hundred years, but do you know what I did on Presidents' Day?

Of course you don't, because I didn't tell you yet. And I'm not going to tell you.

Okay, okay, I'll tell you. I spent the whole morning working on my Presidents' Day oral report!

See, I *told* you that you wouldn't believe it. But it's true! I did homework on a day we didn't even have school! I must have been out of my mind.

I'll tell you why I did it. It's because I hate Andrea Young. I am sick and tired of her bragging about how smart she is and how she knows everything and how her oral report was going to be the best in the class. I'm just as gifted and talented as *she*

is. So I decided I was going to make a *better* oral report than Andrea. I was going to make the *best* oral report in the history of the world. My oral report was going to blow the doors off Andrea's oral report. So nah-nah-nah boo-boo on her!

I worked really hard. I looked in my library and got books about my president.

I looked in the encyclopedia for my president. I went on the Internet and got lots of fun facts about my president. My oral report was going to be great. Andrea wouldn't even know what hit her.

I wrote the whole thing out and put it in a nice red binder. I wouldn't let anyone see it, not even my parents or my sister. I wanted it to be a *complete* surprise. It was top secret. I'm not even going to tell *you* who my president was. So nah-nah-nah boo-boo on you!

I worked all morning on my oral report, and then the phone rang. My mom told me Michael wanted to talk to me.

"Me and my dad are going to buy a big-screen TV," he said. "Wanna come?"

"Sure!"

Michael's dad drove us to the big-screen TV store. It was cool. They had a whole wall filled with big-screen TVs, and they were all tuned to the same channel. We were walking around looking for a salesman when this guy asked Michael's dad if he needed any help. You'll never in a million hundred years believe who the guy was.

I'm not going to tell you.

Okay, okay, I'll tell you.

It was Mr. Macky! He was wearing a name tag that said HOWARD MACKY on it.

"Mr. Macky!" I said. "To what do we

owe the pleasure of your company?"

"I work here on weekends and holidays," said Mr. Macky. "Would you like to buy a big-screen TV? They're on sale today."

Wow! I never would have thought that a *reading specialist* would also be a big-screen TV salesman. I thought reading specialists *hated* TV. But Mr. Macky told us he loved TV and knew everything about big-screen TVs.

Mr. Macky took a *Star Wars* DVD out of his pocket so we could see what it looked like on a big-screen TV. It was cool. You could almost see inside Darth Vader's nostrils.

Michael's dad bought the TV right away. It was so big that Mr. Macky had to help us strap it to the roof of the car.

I asked Mr. Macky what his favorite part of *Star Wars* was. He told us it was the beginning, when all those words scroll up the screen.

"That's the only part you read," he said. "As you know, I love to read."

Mr. Macky is weird. And he is much better at selling TVs than he is at teaching reading.

The President Is Missing!

The next day we had to go to school (BOO!), but we also got to give our oral reports (YAY!). It was cool watching everybody walk up the front steps dressed up like a president. Kids were wearing hats, beards, suits, and ties. Even the girls! That was weird.

Neil the nude kid was dressed up like Thomas Jefferson. He brought his ferret, Mr. Wiggles—I mean *President* Wiggles— with him in a cage. Neil told us that President Wiggles was going to sit in Mr. Klutz's office all day and boss him around because he was president of the school.

Ryan was dressed up like James Garfield, and he brought a stuffed Garfield cat with him. Michael was dressed up like Herbert Hoover, and he brought a vacuum cleaner with him.

"Which president are you, A.J.?" they asked when they saw me. I had a cane, glasses, and a fur hat.

"It's a secret," I said. "But just watch me blow the doors off Andrea's oral report."

After we pledged the allegiance in our class, Mrs. Patty's voice came over the loudspeaker. She told us Mr. Klutz had an announcement to make.

"Two very special guests are visiting our school today," he said. "Dr. Carbles, the president of the Board of Education, will be here any minute. He is eager to

hear some of your Presidents' Day oral reports. And I would like to welcome the new president of Ella Mentry School . . . Mr. Wiggles, the ferret that belongs to Neil Crouch in Miss Daisy's class!"

Everybody started cheering. Neil the nude kid took a bow. This song called "Hail to the Chief" came out of the loudspeaker. When it was over, Mr. Klutz and Mrs. Patty were still talking. I guess they forgot to turn off the microphone in the office.

"Uh, where's the ferret?" Mr. Klutz asked.

"I don't know."

"I thought you had it."

"I put the cage on your desk."

"I put it on the floor over there."

"The cage is empty!" shouted Mrs. Patty. "The ferret must have escaped!"

"Oh no!"

"Mr. Wiggles!" screamed Neil the nude kid.

He totally freaked and went running out of the class. Meanwhile, Mr. Klutz and Mrs. Patty were still talking over the loudspeaker.

"We have to find the ferret!" shouted Mr. Klutz.

"It must

be around here somewhere!"

"How far could a ferret get?"

"It could be anywhere!"

"We'll have to search the school!"

"Lock the outside doors!" shouted Mr. Klutz. "Don't tell the students that the ferret is missing! They might freak out!"

But it was too late. By now *everybody* knew that President Wiggles was missing, and *everybody* was freaking out. Miss Daisy told us to stay in our seats, but there was no way I was going to stay in my seat with a ferret running around loose. Those things look like long rats! It could be in my desk for all I knew.

We all went running into the hallway, and guess who we saw there?

I'm not going to tell you.

Okay, okay, I'll tell you. It was Dr. Carbles, the president of the Board of Education!

"What's going on here?" asked Dr. Carbles. Unlike Dr. Seuss, he's a real doctor, but he isn't very cool.

We couldn't tell him what was going on, because the whole school was going crazy. Kids dressed up like presidents were spilling out of classrooms and running all over the hall, shouting and smashing into one another.

"Help!" somebody screamed. "There's a wild ferret on the loose!"

"Run for your lives!"

"Find the ferret!"

Mr. Macky was shouting at us, trying to control the situation.

"Everyone back to your classes!" he yelled. "Please remain calm!"

Calm? Was he nuts? There was a *ferret* running around the school!

Somebody knocked over Dr. Carbles. The teachers were yelling for us to go back to class. If President Wiggles was smart, he would have found a good hiding place where he wouldn't get trampled by some kid.

Meanwhile, me and Ryan and Michael were sneaking around like Secret Service agents on the hunt for President Wiggles.

It was cool. You should have been there.

President Wiggles, Reporting for Doody

Well, we searched all over the school, but we just couldn't find President Wiggles. When we finally returned to our class, everybody was looking around the room. President Wiggles could be *anywhere*. Poor Neil the nude kid was really upset. If his ferret was lost, his parents were going

to be mad.

Miss Daisy said President Wiggles was sure to turn up and we had to get back to work. It was time for us to give our oral reports. Little Miss Perfect Andrea got to go first. She was dressed up like John F. Kennedy.

"'Ask not what your country can do for you,'" Andrea said. "'Ask what *you* can do for your country.'"

I had to admit that Andrea's oral report

was pretty good. She told us that John F. Kennedy was a war hero and that he started the space program and the Peace Corps. He was cool.

"Exemplary!" Miss Daisy said as Andrea walked back to her seat. (That means "excellent" in grown-up talk.)

"Wait until you hear *my* oral report," I whispered to Ryan. "I'm gonna blow Andrea's doors off."

Next it was crybaby Emily's turn. She was dressed up like Abraham Lincoln with a suit, tie, big black hat, and fake beard.

Emily's report was really sad. She told us that Abraham Lincoln was dirt poor as a kid, his three-year-old son died, his wife went crazy, and the country was at war with itself the whole time he was president. And then, to top it all off, a few days after the war ended, some guy shot him.

Emily started coughing and rubbing her eyes like she was going to cry. For once I couldn't call her a crybaby. The story of Abraham Lincoln was really sad. Andrea was crying. Miss Daisy was crying. Then Michael and Ryan started crying, too. *Everybody* was crying. Even *me*!

While we were all crying, the most amazing thing in the history of the world happened. The big Lincoln hat on Emily's head started moving around. It was like it had a motor in it or something. And then the front of the hat lifted up a little. And you know what was under there?

I'm not going to tell you.

Okay, okay, I'll tell you.

It was President Wiggles! He was sitting on top of Emily's head!

"EEEEEEEEEEEEEEK!" Emily screamed. "THERE'S A RAT IN MY HAT!* I THINK IT JUST POOPED IN MY HAIR!"

Emily totally freaked and ran out of the room. President Wiggles jumped off her head and ran away. Neil the nude kid chased him around the class.

It was hilarious. A real Kodak moment. And we got to see it live and in person!

---

*Isn't that the name of a Dr. Seuss book? I think Miss Daisy read us that book. It was cool.

My Turn at Last

Just when it was my turn to give my oral report, Mr. Macky came into our class. *Good*, I thought. I wanted him to see me blow the doors off Andrea.

I took my report and went to the front of the room with my cane and glasses and fur hat.

"My name is Benjamin Franklin," I read from my report. "I'm on the hundred-dollar bill, and I lived a very interesting life."

I told the class all the cool stuff I learned about Benjamin Franklin. Like how he ran away from home when he was a teenager. And how he became a famous printer and

writer. And how he became a famous inventor and discovered that lightning was electricity. And how he helped to write the Declaration of Independence and the Constitution. And how he turned three hundred years old in 2006.

Everybody was totally silent while I read my awesome oral report, so I knew it must have been really good. I was blowing Andrea's doors off! Nah-nah-nah boo-boo on her!

Finally I came to the last line of my report. I looked up. Everybody was staring at me. They had weird looks on their faces.

"What's wrong?" I asked.

Andrea was the only one who said

anything.

"Benjamin Franklin wasn't even a president, dumbhead."

"Huh?" I said.

I looked at Mr. Macky. I was sure he was going to tell little Miss Smarty Pants that she was wrong and that she should keep her big mouth shut. She doesn't know everything.

But he didn't.

"A.J.," Mr. Macky said, "Benjamin Franklin was a great man, but he was never president of the United States."

He *wasn't*? I read a lot of stuff about Benjamin Franklin. It never said he *wasn't* president. I just figured he *had* to be a president. Why would they put him on a hundred-dollar bill if he wasn't even a president?

I didn't know what to say. I didn't know what to do. I had to think fast.

So I said the only thing I could say.

"I knew that!"

Then I did the only thing I could do.

I ran out of the room. And I'm never going back.

I'm going to Antarctica to live with the penguins. Penguins are cool. And it won't matter to them that I did my Presidents' Day oral report on a guy who wasn't even a president.

Maybe Neil the nude kid will catch President Wiggles. Maybe Mr. Macky will become a full-time big-screen TV salesman. Maybe Abraham Lincoln will beat up George Washington. Maybe Mr. Klutz will grow some hair on his head so I can write a Dr. Seuss poem about it. Maybe I'll come back in time for Presidents' Day next year, when everybody will have forgotten my dumb report. Or maybe I can find a way to get Benjamin Franklin elected president of the United States even though he's been dead since 1790.

But it won't be easy!

Check out the My Weird School series!

#1: Miss Daisy Is Crazy!
Pb 0-06-050700-4
The first book in the hilarious series stars A.J., a second grader who hates school—and can't believe his teacher hates it too!

#2: Mr. Klutz Is Nuts!
Pb 0-06-050702-0
A.J. can't believe his crazy principal wants to climb to the top of the flagpole!

#3: Mrs. Roopy Is Loopy!
Pb 0-06-050704-7
The new librarian at A.J.'s weird school thinks she's George Washington one day and Little Bo Peep the next!

#4: Ms. Hannah Is Bananas!
Pb 0-06-050706-3
Ms. Hannah, the art teacher, wears clothes made from pot holders. Worse than that, she's trying to make A.J. be partners with yucky Andrea!

#5: Miss Small Is off the Wall!
Pb 0-06-074518-5
Miss Small, the gym teacher, is teaching A.J.'s class to juggle scarves, balance feathers, and do everything *but* play sports!

#6: Mr. Hynde Is Out of His Mind!
Pb 0-06-074520-7
The music teacher, Mr. Hynde, plays bongo drums on the principal's bald head! But does he have what it takes to be a real rock-and-roll star?

#7: Mrs. Cooney Is Loony!
Pb 0-06-074522-3
Mrs. Cooney, the school nurse, is everybody's favorite—but is she hiding a secret identity?

#8: Ms. LaGrange Is Strange!
Pb 0-06-082223-6
The new lunch lady, Ms. LaGrange, talks funny—and why is she writing secret messages in the mashed potatoes?

#9: Miss Lazar Is Bizarre!
Pb 0-06-082225-2

What kind of grown-up *likes* cleaning throw-up? Miss Lazar is the weirdest custodian in the history of the world!

#10: Mr. Docker Is off His Rocker!
Pb 0-06-082227-9

Mr. Docker, the science teacher, alarms and amuses A.J.'s class with his wacky experiments and nutty inventions.

#11: Mrs. Kormel Is Not Normal!
Pb 0-06-082229-5

A.J.'s school bus gets a flat tire, then becomes hopelessly lost at the hands of Mrs. Kormel, the wacky bus driver.

#12: Ms. Todd Is Odd!
Pb 0-06-082231-7

Ms. Todd is subbing, and A.J. and his friends are sure she kidnapped Miss Daisy so she could take over her job.

#13: Mrs. Patty Is Batty!
Pb 0-06-085380-8

In this special Halloween installment, a little bit of spookiness and a lot of humor add up to the best trick-or-treating adventure ever!

#14: Miss Holly Is Too Jolly!
Pb 0-06-085382-4

When Miss Holly starts hanging mistletoe around the classroom, A.J. knows to watch out. Because mistletoe means kissletoe, the worst holiday tradition in the history of the world!

Also look for
#16 Ms. Coco Is Loco!

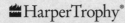

HarperTrophy®
An Imprint of HarperCollins*Publishers*

www.harpercollinschildrens.com   **www.dangutman.com**